To the Rescue

Jason was pushing Ernest back toward the brick school wall. The black commando grease stripes left from the night before made Jason's face look more evil than ever. Ernest was so scared that he accidentally swallowed his gum.

All at once, the pushing stopped. Jason stood motionless.

There was Jomo, his face grim and threatening. He stood between Ernest and the wall, staring directly into Jason's eyes. "Cut it out!" he said in a low, menacing voice. . . .

How To Survive Third Grade

LAURIE LAWLOR

**Illustrated by
Joyce Audy Zarins**

A MINSTREL® BOOK

PUBLISHED BY POCKET BOOKS

New York   London   Toronto   Sydney   Tokyo   Singapore

With special thanks to Matt Banic of Rochester, Indiana,
and his cow, Wilma

A Minstrel Book published by
POCKET BOOKS, a division of Simon & Schuster Inc.
1230 Avenue of the Americas, New York, NY 10020

Text copyright © 1988 by Laurie Lawlor
Illustrations copyright © 1988 by Joyce Audy Zarins
Cover artwork © 1991 by Tim Galasinski

ISBN: 0-671-67713-6

First Minstrel Books printing January 1991

10 9 8 7 6 5

A MINSTREL BOOK and colophon are registered trademarks
of Simon & Schuster Inc.

Printed in U.S.A.

For Jack and his model airplanes

CHAPTER

1

More than anything, Ernest wished he could fly. He even had dreams of running across the muddy playground at Lincoln School, leaping higher and higher until, with one gigantic jump, he was soaring. The nasty third graders on the ground below looked as tiny as bugs. They couldn't reach him. He was flying over autumn-bright trees, over the clouds, with his arms outstretched and the wind in his hair.

"Maybe someday." Ernest sighed as he pushed away his bowl of breakfast cereal. The fat orange tabby cat jumped on the cluttered table and lapped up the milk and the last soggy Cheerios. "Help yourself, Dash," Ernest said. He looked again at the note his mother had hastily written before she left for work.

Ernie honey—
Will be late tonight from office. Don't forget
to lock the door. Call me when you get home.
Do your homework. Feed the cat. Do not turn
on the stove. Do not answer the phone or the
doorbell.

Love,
Mom

Letting himself in and out of the house with his own key had been Ernest's idea. Now that he was a third grader, he could save them money. His mother wouldn't have to pay a neighbor to watch him before and after school anymore.

He did not mind being left alone. What bothered him were his mother's daily messages. They always said the same thing. Didn't she trust him? He had been using his own key for more than a month, ever since third grade started. Most of the time he managed to remember his homework, and he always fed the cat. He never turned on the stove, and he never forgot to call his mother. And who would telephone or come to visit while she was away at work? Certainly no one very interesting. He had no friends.

He longed desperately to have a best friend or kind-of-sort-of best friend or even someone just to walk to school with. But somehow, in Mrs. Delacorte's class, Ernest always managed to blurt out the wrong thing or pick his nose when someone was looking or answer a question stupidly or fumble the ball in gym and lose the third-grade championship kickball game.

It didn't help that he was unusually small for his age and that the economical haircuts his mother insisted on giving him always made his head look pointed. Someday, he hoped, he could wear something besides his cousins' frayed hand-me-downs. Perhaps someday his mother would buy him the kind of gym shoes the other third graders wore, not the kindergarten kind with rubber toes and no bright laces. Maybe then people would like him. Maybe then someone would invite him to come over after school and play Monopoly or watch television or eat snacks the way he imagined best friends did.

Ernest glanced at the kitchen clock. He had less than five minutes to get to school on time. He pulled on his coat, grabbed his sack lunch, math book, and the notebook he always carried for sketching and doodling, and bolted outside. It was raining hard.

He was halfway down the block when he remembered that he had not shut the basement door. What if Dash went downstairs and made a mess of his model airplane collection, the most precious thing he owned? He'd never forgive himself if something happened to the sleek new model of the F-5F Tiger II fighter plane he was finishing.

Ernest ran back into the house, found Dash safe in the kitchen, and slammed the basement door hard. His soaked baseball jacket stuck to his back, and the damp edges of his homework pages began to curl as he searched the closet for last year's raincoat. He thrust his arms in the sleeves and discovered a huge rip. An umbrella! If only he could find an umbrella, maybe he wouldn't have to apologize again to Mrs. Delacorte for soggy homework. Ernest rummaged through the closet on his hands and knees, but the only umbrella he could find belonged to his mother. It was pink with big red roses.

He hesitated. What if someone saw him?

The street looked empty. He decided he'd race all the way with the umbrella and hide it somewhere as soon as he got to the playground. No one would ever know he had carried anything that so obviously belonged to a girl.

Just as he reached the school fence, he heard the last warning bell. He was tardy again! Breathlessly, he ran to the main entrance. The fifth-grade crossing guards were wandering in from helping kindergartners and first graders cross the streets.

"Hey, Runt! Where'd you get that umbrella? From your grandmother?" one hooted.

Ernest struggled to collapse the monstrous pink thing and hide it inside his jacket as a crowd of classmates from Room 203 thundered past. But it was no use. He had been discovered. There stood Jason Sweeny, the worst third grader who ever lived. Ernest felt his face blush as bright red as the roses.

"Give it to me, Ernie!" Jason screamed in a high-pitched voice. "I don't want to get my hairdo wet!"

"Ah, shut up!" Ernest hissed angrily.

"Don't get mad, Teeny-Weeny," said Jason's friend Etherial. "Just hand it over!"

"No!"

Jason and his sidekicks grabbed the umbrella,

laughing and yelling. They ran upstairs to the third-grade classrooms. Ernest would have caught up with them except that he dropped his homework. Pages went flying. By the time he picked everything up, the boys were at the top of the stairs, tossing the umbrella back and forth.

"Cooties! Cooties!"

"Touch this and you'll have cooties, too!"

"What's going on here?" Mrs. Delacorte's voice boomed. "Get your coats in your lockers and come into the classroom quietly, or I'll send you to the principal's office."

As soon as Mrs. Delacorte went into the classroom, Ernest's mother's umbrella rocketed overhead and landed on the ledge above the lockers. Ernest jumped, but he could not reach it. Jason and his friends snickered and slunk into Room 203.

"Ernest, is something wrong?" Mrs. Delacorte asked in a kind voice.

"No, ma'am," Ernest said as he sat down at his desk. He was thankful she didn't call him Ernie, even when he stayed after school to work with her on his math. He hated that name.

"Are you sure you're OK?"

Ernest nodded. He could never explain about the hideous umbrella. It would be too humiliating. All he could think of was the awful summer he turned five. His mother had thoughtlessly told one of their neighbors that he liked to sleep in an old shirt that had once belonged to his cousin Theresa. It was just a big, comfortable T-shirt really, but practically every kid on the block teased him for months. "Ernie wears a nightgown! Ernie wears a nightgown!"

He could still hear their voices. If he told his teacher about the pink rose umbrella, he knew he'd be made fun of for the rest of his life.

"All right. Now, class," Mrs. Delacorte announced, "I want all of you to listen carefully. If it stops raining this afternoon, we will be having our Lincoln School Balloon Send-off. Many of you probably remember this event from last year. I'll be handing out postcards for you to write your name, your grade, and the name and address of our school. You'll attach your cards to the strings of helium balloons and let the balloons go at exactly the same moment. We hope that whoever finds the cards will write back."

Sheila raised her hand. "What's the prize this year for the one that goes the farthest?"

"Mr. Momaday says the winner and a friend of his or her choice will receive a free dinner at Pizza Roma."

The class cheered. For once, their principal had had a good idea.

"All the pizza you can eat?" Ben demanded, resting his plump chin on one hand.

Mrs. Delacorte laughed. "We'll see about that. Now I'd like you to get out your math homework and pass it to the front of your row."

Ernest tried to smooth his wet, crushed paper but only managed to smear the penciled columns of numbers. He stared out the window and remembered how beautiful all three hundred balloons of every color had looked last year, floating up into the sky. It had been a thrilling sight.

No one ever wrote to say they had found his balloon's card. But he could still imagine the journey his balloon might have taken.

Ernest wished he could send himself instead of a card. In his notebook, he sketched balloons sailing high over the lake on a good strong wind, maybe all the way to Michigan. He slid back in his seat, daydreaming.

The clear lake breeze and cloudless sky suddenly vanished. There was frowning Mrs. Delacorte, her feet planted squarely on the linoleum. She was pointing to a number line. "Ernest, please pay attention. I'll repeat the question. What is negative one plus positive one?"

"I . . . don't know," Ernest mumbled.

"Zero," somebody whispered. "Just like Teeny-Weeny's brain."

Ernest kept his eyes down. He found it helped if he didn't look directly at anyone when he was embarrassed.

Mrs. Delacorte glanced at Ernest's desk before he could shut his notebook with all his detailed sketches. "Ernest, please remember this is math, not art class."

"Sorry," Ernest said. Quickly, he slipped his math book over the drawing of his father in the cockpit of a MIG-23. On paper, Ernest's father was an ace fighter pilot in a Navy and Air Force Aggressor Squadron. In real life, however, he didn't fly planes. He installed mufflers in California.

Ernest's parents had been divorced since he was a baby, and he only heard from his father on his birthday. Ernest had plenty of time the rest of the year to invent him a much more glamorous career, flying fighter jets faster than the speed of sound.

But this morning Ernest couldn't concentrate on military aircraft or his imaginary father. He couldn't pay attention to anything Mrs. Delacorte was saying. A big worry gnawed at him. How was he ever going to reach the umbrella stuck on the hallway ledge? His mother would be furious when she discovered the umbrella was missing. "Ernest," he could hear her demanding, "why in the world do you let those boys take advantage of you? Can't you do anything right?"

Of course, she wouldn't listen to his side of the story. She had no idea what it was like being the most unpopular third grader at Lincoln School.

In the margin of his notebook, Ernest scribbled a picture of himself. He was hanging dangerously upside down by one foot from the handle of an open umbrella.

CHAPTER

2

The rain stopped. The playground equipment glistened in the sunshine as if it were freshly painted. Inside the gym, the mothers from the PTA were chattering and filling balloons with a helium tank. WHOOSH! WHOOSH! The balloon send-off would take place that afternoon as planned, right before lunch recess. Mrs. Delacorte's class was excited.

"I hope I win," Ben said dreamily. "I'll order an El Supremo. Cheese, sausage, pepperoni, bacon, green peppers, onions, and anchovies."

"If I win," Sheila announced, "I just don't know which of my best, best friends I'll invite. I've got *so-o-o* many, you know."

Ernest didn't say anything. He wanted his balloon to go the farthest, too. The only problem was, whom would he invite to go out for pizza if he won? He couldn't go alone, and he certainly couldn't take his mother. Everyone would laugh at him.

There was a knock at the classroom door. Mrs. Delacorte disappeared into the hallway for several minutes. Everyone wanted to know what was taking so long.

"She's talking to the principal!"

"What are they saying?"

"I can't hear anything!"

When Mrs. Delacorte returned, she was followed by a boy no one had ever seen before. Even though he was tall and muscular, he seemed painfully shy. He kept his eyes on the floor so that he would not have to meet any of the other students' questioning stares. Ernest wondered if the boy felt out of place because of his odd clothing. He was the only student in Room 203 wearing khaki shorts, long, thick socks, and strange-looking sandals. The new boy's spotless white shirt with its stiff collar and little embroidered design on the pocket made his deep black skin look even darker.

"Class," Mrs. Delacorte said, "this is our new student. He is joining us at Lincoln School all the way from Kenya. I want you to welcome Jomo Mugwana."

The new boy looked up for an instant when he heard his name. He nodded but did not smile.

"What kind of a weird name is Jomo?" Sheila's friend, Emily, whispered.

"He sure doesn't look very friendly," Ben remarked.

"We all have to be especially helpful to Jomo over the next few months," Mrs. Delacorte continued. "He knows very little English yet. With all of our help, he will learn quickly. Jomo is from a country in eastern Africa." She pulled down the map above the blackboard to show the class just how far Jomo had traveled. "Almost halfway around the world—maybe even farther than any of our balloons will travel this afternoon."

The class laughed. Jomo looked confused.

"Please take the seat over here next to Ernest, Jomo," Mrs. Delacorte said, leading him to an empty desk. Jomo sat down.

Ernest smiled at the new boy, wondering if his

clothes were the kind African students wore. Jomo's hands were folded together very tightly on top of his desk, and he kept nervously biting his lower lip. Ernest knew just how uncomfortable he must be feeling. It was nerve-wracking having everyone look at you as if you were from another planet.

"Please get out a pencil and fill in your balloon send-off cards," Mrs. Delacorte said. "I will help anyone who raises his or her hand."

Ernest watched Jomo from the corner of his eye. The new boy's hands were still folded. He had no card, and he did not know what he was supposed to do. Ernest opened his desk, took out an extra pencil, and gave his card to Jomo. "Write your name here," Ernest whispered.

Jomo did not understand. Ernest tried using sign language. He pointed at Jomo. He pointed at the pencil and pretended to write on the card. Jomo shrugged.

Ernest took out a piece of paper and drew a picture of a balloon floating up into the sky. On one end of the string he drew a rectangle. He put his finger on the card and then on the rectangle in the picture. Jomo still looked puzzled.

This was harder than Ernest had imagined it would be. "Me," he said, patting himself and taking back the card, "Ernest. E-R-N-E-S-T. See? I write it like this. OK?" Jomo watched Ernest write and then erase his name. "You, Jomo. J-O-M-O. Write it on the card. OK?"

Jomo held the pencil and the card but did not write anything. Ernest took a deep breath and raised his hand. "Mrs. Delacorte, I think Jomo needs your help."

"Thank you for trying," she said, giving Ernest a new card. Quickly, she wrote Jomo's name for him.

"Ernie, did you give him your pencil, too?" Jason asked in a low voice.

"Oh, no! Ernie gave the new guy his booger pencil!" Etherial shrieked.

Someone laughed.

"Poor Jomo."

Ernest tried to ignore his classmates' comments while he filled out the new card. He was glad when the class went down to the gym to pick out balloons.

Blue. He had already decided his balloon would be the color of the sky. Blue was his lucky color.

Mrs. Delacorte handed Jomo a red balloon and attached his card for him. "Hold onto this, Jomo," she said. Jomo followed her outside with the rest of the class.

CHAPTER
3

The entire school waited on the playground for Mr. Momaday to announce the moment of the balloon send-off on his bullhorn. The principal seemed to be stalling. There was a rumor that a television camera crew might film the send-off. Everyone knew Mr. Momaday wanted to be on television. He had autographed copies of local TV celebrities on the walls in his office. "To Leon," one of them said. "Sorry I couldn't visit Lincoln School in person. Don't give up your dream of being in broadcasting."

Mr. Momaday looked at his watch and sighed. No one from WBON-TV would be coming, after all. And the crowd was getting restless. A few of the older boys were running around trying to pop each other's balloons.

"Ready?" Mr. Momaday finally shouted. "One,

two, three! Let go of your balloons, and GOOD LUCK!"

The balloons rose like a colorful cloud. Ernest's blue balloon danced for a moment in a gust of wind. Suddenly, it headed straight for a tree branch. He watched in shock as the lucky blue balloon exploded.

Everyone else was cheering and jumping up and down, looking at the sky. Ernest wiped his eyes with the sleeve of his jacket. He felt terrible.

"Is anything the matter, Ernest?" Mrs. Delacorte asked.

Ernest pointed to the tree. "Mine popped."

"That's too bad. I'll get you another. There seem to be plenty."

Ernest dug his toe into the damp ground. He was glad Mrs. Delacorte understood. He was glad he didn't have to explain how disappointed he felt when the balloon broke. She might think he was acting like a baby.

"Here you go, Ernest," she said quietly, handing him a card, a pencil, and a new balloon. "I hope yellow will do."

Ernest smiled. "Sure. Yellow's fine. Thanks." He

scribbled the information quickly and let the balloon go. "Goodbye! Good luck!" he whispered, watching the balloon become a smaller and smaller dot until it disappeared.

Someone was poking his back. Ernest whirled around, expecting Jason or one of the other third-grade bullies. But it was Jomo. He was trying to return Ernest's pencil.

"How did you like the balloon send-off?" Ernest asked, making upward motions with his arms. "Wasn't it great?"

From his back pocket, Jomo pulled the picture of the balloon Ernest had drawn. He pointed to the sky. He pointed to the picture.

And for the first time, Jomo smiled.

Ernest felt very happy. Even though he and Jomo spoke different languages, they understood each other. He wondered if this was what it felt like to have a friend—you understood what the other person meant without using any words at all.

Ernest's mind raced. Maybe he and Jomo could be friends. Maybe they could do things like walk home from school together. Maybe he could even show Jomo his airplanes.

Just as Ernest was about to sketch Jomo a picture of his newest model on the back of the balloon drawing, a group of boys surrounded them.

"They play soccer in your country?"

"Come on, Jomo! Play ball with us!"

A soccer ball flew high in the air and bounced on someone's knee. When the ball landed on the ground, Jomo made a deadly pivot kick that shot it past Jason.

"The new kid's too fast for you, Jason!"

"Jomo, you're good!"

"Yeah, Jason, better watch out!" someone howled.

"Be on my team!"

"Don't stand around talking to Ernie. He's just a runt. Play with us."

The boys raced into the field after the ball. Jomo laughed and followed them.

Ernest watched sadly as the boys began practicing passes, shouting and calling to one another. Jomo was someone new from a faraway, exciting country. He was good at sports. Soon everyone would like him. They would try to sit next to him at lunch. They would ask to help him with his math homework. They would give him birthday invitations.

Now Ernest knew that he and Jomo could never be friends. Once Jomo learned English, the others would tell him stories about Ernest. Jomo would learn all their hateful habits, their horrid lies. He would think as badly of Ernest as everyone else did.

Ernest put his hands in his pockets and walked slowly back into the school building. He wondered if the rest of his life would feel as lonely as this very moment.

CHAPTER

4

After school ended that day, Ernest lingered in the hallway. Everyone except Mrs. Delacorte had left. His plan was simple. He would wait until she, too, went home, and then he would climb on top of the custodian's big garbage can to retrieve his mother's umbrella.

"Ernest?" Mrs. Delacorte called. "Do you have a moment?"

Ernest stood shyly in the doorway. His teacher was holding the F-5F Tiger II with two sidewinder missiles he had drawn in art class a week ago. "This is very good, Ernest. I've noticed you've drawn a number of airplanes and jets during free time. You're quite an artist."

He shrugged in embarrassment. No one had ever called him an artist before.

"Do you think you'd like to be featured in the Expert Club's Collection display case in the hall? We could put up all your sketches, maybe some more you may have done at home—"

"No. Thank you, but no," Ernest interrupted. He was horrified. The last thing he wanted was for the whole school to make fun of him *and* his pictures. Drawing and making airplane models was very private, very special. What if people laughed at his drawings?

Mrs. Delacorte looked confused. "I only thought you might enjoy seeing your work on display."

"No, I . . . really don't want to. No."

"I see. Well, maybe someday. It's still a fine drawing."

"Thanks. You can keep it," Ernest said quickly.

"I'd like that, Ernest. It's very nice. Are you on your way home now?"

"Um, yes."

"That's good. Ernest, don't dilly-dally. Good night."

"Good night," Ernest replied. He walked down

the hall as if he were leaving. When Mrs. Delacorte wasn't looking, he dove behind a big garbage can and watched his teacher turn off the classroom lights, lock the door, and go downstairs.

At last he was alone. Ernest pushed the big garbage can against the row of lockers. He climbed carefully on top, trying to keep his feet near the rim where the plastic lid seemed thickest. He grabbed the umbrella.

"Hey, kid! What are you doing up here?" a custodian shouted.

The sound startled Ernest. He lost his balance and stepped on the middle of the lid. The next moment, he was inside the garbage can, covered with pencil shavings and someone's vanilla yogurt from lunch. The umbrella was still clenched in his fist.

"You're lucky you didn't break your neck!" the custodian said. He helped Ernest scramble over the side.

"I was just trying to reach—"

"First graders have no business up here. Don't you know this floor's for third, fourth, and fifth graders? Now get downstairs and get home."

Ernest blushed. It was a good thing no one else

was around to hear him being called a first grader. Without answering, he ran down the steps and out of the school.

He did not stop running until he came to his front door. Then Ernest caught his breath, relieved that he had been able to retrieve the umbrella. His mother would never have to know what had happened at school.

He turned the key. As soon as he was inside, he hurled the hateful pink monster into the closet and slammed the door tight. The umbrella was back where it belonged.

"Hello, Dash," he said, petting the cat that lovingly circled his leg. "Miss me?"

Ernest telephoned a message for his mother at A-1 Plate Glass Company to say he had arrived home safely. Because she would be home later than usual, he made himself a big snack: cold pizza from the refrigerator. He broke off a corner for the cat and took the rest downstairs.

Dash, who was particularly fond of cheese and sausage, followed Ernest into his basement workroom that smelled of airplane enamel, model cement, and the old, musty newspapers that lined the table and shelves. This was the one place in the whole world where Ernest felt completely comfortable, completely safe.

Colorful plastic jets and bombers, gliders, and prop planes hung from the ceiling on pieces of fishing line. There was a whole fleet of miniature Freedom Fighters parked in a neat row on one shelf. Ernest liked to think he had made a model of almost every different jet fighter that ever flew.

He opened the basement window so there would be plenty of fresh air while he worked. The aircraft hanging from the ceiling moved ever so slightly in the breeze as if they might actually take off and begin flying all by themselves.

At the table cluttered with sandpaper, small knives, tweezers, glass paint bottles, tubes of glue, and slender paintbrushes was his favorite model, the half-finished F-5F Tiger II. He had been carefully assembling the elegant, pointed air-to-air fighter for almost a week. It was a real beauty designed to fly faster than any of its predecessors. Improvements included a two-position nose-gear strut for better take-off, an arrestor hook, maneuvering flaps, a bigger fuel tank, and increased wing

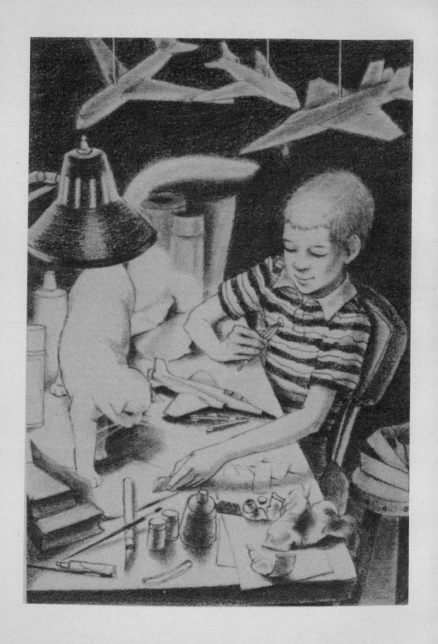

area. The 20mm cannon and sidewinder missiles looked very authentic.

The man at the hobby store had warned Ernest that the model might be too difficult for someone his age. Even the box said the model was "recommended for experienced modelers age 12 and older."

Ernest smiled. The F-5F Tiger II had been challenging, but not impossible. And he had done it all by himself. With the tip of his finger, he made sure the paintbrush strokes were even and smooth. He was proud that he always painted in the same direction.

Peering through the clear canopy into one of the cockpits, Ernest imagined himself and his co-pilot in the tiny seats. He pretended he was at the controls, steering the plane down the runway into a perfect take-off. He carefully lifted the F-5F Tiger II fuselage and watched it soar six thousand miles over the Atlantic—all the way to Africa.

CHAPTER

5

"Mine went farthest at last year's send-off. I bet you anything it does again," Sheila bragged the next day. The class was waiting for Mrs. Delacorte to return from the media center with their film on the life cycle of a honeybee. Jason and Etherial were making spitballs on the radiator.

"Your balloon didn't go the farthest in the whole school. Just in the second grade," Ben corrected her between mouthfuls of lunch. He always hid his bologna sandwich inside his desk in case he was in the mood for a snack.

"Yeah, Sheila-bobeela-nana-fana-fofeela, a fifth grader won the prize last year. My cousin knew him." Jason batted a handful of spitballs across the room with his ruler.

"Cut it out!" Ernest complained. A big, wet spit-ball had lodged itself in the spiral binding of his notebook.

"What's the matter, Teeny-Weeny? Afraid of a little spitball?"

Ernest didn't say anything. Sometimes ignoring Jason was the safest thing to do. He closed his notebook and looked at Jomo. There was a spitball on Jomo's desk, too. Jomo stared hard at Jason, his dark eyes looking even darker.

"Now Africa man's mad. Better watch out," said Etherial.

"Why don't you shut up, Etherial?" Emily replied.

"Yeah, it isn't fair," Ben agreed. "Jomo doesn't even know English."

"What do they speak in his country, anyhow? Monkey talk? Ooh-Ooh-AH-AH-Ooh-Ooh-AH-AH!" Jason made chimpanzee noises.

"Cut it out," Ernest said again in a small voice.

Jason batted three more spitballs across the room. One hit Jomo squarely on the arm. Jomo brushed it off and stood up. This was exactly what Jason wanted. He bounded across the room to

Jomo, pretending to be a karate expert.

"I'm going to tell Mrs. Delacorte," Sheila announced.

Nobody cared. The class was on its feet now for a better look. What would Jomo do?

Jason hooted and made some extra fancy kicks in the air. "Come on, Jumbo!"

"I bet he's a chicken," Etherial said.

"He's afraid of you," another one of Jason's henchmen jeered. The bunch gathered around the fight seemed to agree.

Ernest watched in disbelief. Maybe Jomo wasn't as popular as he had thought. Maybe there was a chance the new boy could still be his friend if nobody else liked him.

Jomo pointed at the two spitballs clinging to his desk. He grabbed Jason by the shirt and pulled him over. With one hand, he pushed his face into the spitballs. Jason's arms went flying, but he managed to wriggle free. He bounded back, fists clenched. He made a good left jab that knocked Jomo down.

Jason's face was flushed and angry. He danced around Jomo. Jomo jumped up. He moved swiftly behind Jason, grabbed him by both arms, and held him tight. Jason was surprised by Jomo's strength. He couldn't move.

"Let go!" Jason gasped. "You're gonna break my arms off!"

Jomo would not let go.

"I told you that African kid might be dangerous," Sheila said.

"Yeah, he has a violent face," Emily agreed.

Suddenly, the door to the classroom burst open. Everyone except Jomo and Jason scattered back to their seats. "What in heaven's name is going on here?" Mrs. Delacorte demanded.

"He's trying to kill me!" Jason whimpered.

"Let him go, Jomo!" Mrs. Delacorte ordered.

Jomo could see his teacher was angry. He released Jason's arms. Jason slumped to the floor, groaning and moaning. Mrs. Delacorte was very upset. She was writing something quickly on a piece of paper. "Take this to the principal, Sheila. Both of you boys are going to have to see Mr. Momaday. I am very sorry I cannot trust this class alone for one moment."

Jason groaned loudly and rubbed his arms. "I think he broke something."

"Mrs. Delacorte," Ernest spoke up. "Do you want to know what really—"

Jason gave Ernest a threatening look.

"Not now, Ernest," his teacher interrupted. "I want to get this situation resolved immediately. I will *not* allow fighting in my class."

The room was silent. The class waited breathlessly for the sound of Mr. Momaday's footsteps squeaking down the hall.

"Boys, I think you can both come with me," Mr. Momaday said in his most serious tone from the doorway.

Jason limped out of the room, and Mrs. Delacorte motioned for Jomo to follow him. The door shut.

"I don't know what happened in here just now, but I think discipline for everyone is in order." Mrs. Delacorte nervously tapped her pencil on her desk. "As a result of this incident, there will be no recess today."

The class groaned.

"Why should we get the blame?" someone whispered.

"We *cannot* have this kind of behavior," she continued. "I want you all to think about the way you have been acting lately. We have to learn to get along, to appreciate and respect each other's differences. Jomo doesn't know English. He is from another country, another culture. We must help him. Not fight with him. And even though you were not all involved in what just happened here, you are all partially responsible. You could have stopped the fight."

The class was very disappointed. Mrs. Delacorte's punishment seemed so unfair! Nobody could make Jason do anything he didn't want to do. Because he had repeated first grade, he was the biggest boy in third grade. And his fifth-grade cousins on the playground were even bigger. Jason was always picking on people, trying out what he'd learned at karate lessons. Everyone knew that. Everyone except Mrs. Delacorte.

Soon the classroom door opened. In came Jason, still rubbing his arms. He was followed by Jomo, who meekly took his seat next to Ernest.

It was really too bad, Ernest decided, that Jomo had to get mixed up with someone like Jason. He felt sorry for the new boy. Jomo could hardly speak

English. How could he have known that there were some people at Lincoln School better left alone if he were going to make it to fourth grade alive?

Ernest glanced quickly across the aisle. He wanted to say something. He wanted to whisper to Jomo that everything would be OK, that the fight wasn't his fault. Suddenly, he thought of a plan so bold that it startled him. He'd invite Jomo to his house after school! Then Jomo would understand that at least Ernest Clark still liked him.

Ernest rehearsed his invitation silently. Each time, he became more frightened. He kept thinking of second grade, when he had asked Jimmy Wexler over after school. When Jimmy had shrieked, "No way!" Ernest lost all hope of ever having anyone to his house.

Taking a deep breath, he finally leaned across the aisle. Jomo looked at him, his eyes still angry and betrayed. And in that split second, Ernest forgot everything he was going to say. All he could do was smile weakly. But Jomo did not smile back.

CHAPTER

6

The gray, dreary days of a rainy October seemed to drag on endlessly. There was no word about a balloon send-off winner. Ernest began to wonder if all the balloons had landed in Lake Michigan. None of the students even talked about the free pizza anymore. They were too busy getting ready for Halloween.

On the big day, Mr. Momaday dressed up as a movie star, the way he did every year. His costume was complete with sunglasses and a bright, sequined suit coat. Mrs. Delacorte surprised everyone by wearing a fairy godmother outfit. She even had a magic wand which was really a cardboard star covered in glitter and glued to a stick. Ernest thought she looked very pretty in gauze wings and a cape made of purple netting.

"What this?" Jomo asked his teacher, pointing to her crown of fake diamonds.

"A crown," she said and smiled.

"Crown," Jomo repeated. He seemed puzzled that anything so valuable would be worn by a teacher to school. He added "crown" to his growing list of English words. Jomo was a fast learner. He could even swear now. Every time he swore, the class practically rolled on the floor in delighted laughter. Jomo sounded so funny that they taught him a long list of nasty phrases.

That day, however, Jomo made a mistake. He called Mrs. Delacorte one of the newest swear words he had learned. Everyone giggled uncontrollably.

"Jomo Mugwana, who taught you that?" she demanded, her face nearly as purple as her fancy cape.

Jomo shrugged. Didn't she think he was funny, too?

"You cannot say those words. *Bad* words. Do you understand?"

"OK," Jomo said, nodding uncertainly.

"Class," Mrs. Delacorte continued, trying to

resume a calm expression, "you can now put the finishing touches on your costumes for the All-School Halloween Parade."

There were shrieks and laughter as masks and outfits appeared from inside desks and paper shopping bags. Jomo, who now wore jeans and sweatshirts and gym shoes like everyone else, had learned English well enough to understand Halloween was a time to dress up and go door-to-door demanding candy. He had brought a big floppy hat and a fake beard to school.

"How I look? OK?" he asked Ernest.

"Fine. You look fine, Jomo," Ernest replied. He was glad Jomo seemed to be enjoying himself. This seemed like the perfect moment to go ahead with the new plan he had worked out the night before. He had waited and waited all morning for his chance. At last, when no one seemed to be looking, Ernest gave Jomo a handful of miniature candy bars taken from the freezer at home. His mother had told him to save these treats for the neighborhood children. But Ernest knew best friends shared. He figured sneaking candy was well worth the risk if Jomo would be his friend. "These are pretty good," he said. "Do you like this kind of chocolate?"

Jomo smiled broadly and examined the candies in their bright-colored wrappers. "Tricks or treats!" he said. "Tricks or treats!"

"I wouldn't take that from Ernie if I was you," Etherial murmured. "You might get poisoned."

"Poison?" Jomo replied, looking confused.

Ernest felt himself shrinking. Now everyone was looking at Jomo and the candy. He wished he'd never brought the forbidden chocolates to school. He wished he'd never tried to give them away to someone who didn't understand that Halloween treats were not allowed during class.

"Mrs. Delacorte!" Sheila's voice rang out in piercing sing-song. "Jomo has a bunch of chocolate bars. Didn't you say no candy was allowed?"

"Oh, shut up, Sheila!" Ben grumbled from behind his opened desk lid where he was stuffing one last chocolate kiss into his mouth.

"Jomo, you've heard the rule," Mrs. Delacorte said, motioning with her wand. "No candy until after school. Please step forward and place those Chococrunch bars on my desk."

Reluctantly, Jomo did as he was told. He kept

his eyes lowered and refused to look at anyone as he returned to his seat.

"Germy Ernie Bars," Jason whispered, pretending to choke. The class laughed.

Ernest waved his hand frantically so he could explain that Jomo had done nothing wrong. It was all his fault, not the new boy's.

"We're already late for the All-School Halloween Parade. Your question is going to have to wait, Ernest," Mrs. Delacorte announced, glancing at her watch. "Everyone get in line."

Ernest sighed and slumped down at his desk. He had ruined everything! What if instead of liking him, Jomo hated him? What if he thought Ernest had meant to get him in trouble?

Ernest slowly put on the costume he had worn every Halloween since he was six. It was an old sheet with three holes. He could hear his classmates laughing and joking. They were excited to see all the other kids' outfits. Ernest was not excited in the least. He waited until everyone else was nearly out the door before he joined the others in single file. After two years' experience in the All-School Halloween Parade, he knew the end of the line was the safest place to be. There'd be no third graders behind him to cause trouble.

The parade had circled the playground twice when Ernest's ears rang with the sound of an ominous war whoop. He held his sheet tight under his chin and peered through the big mouth hole at a threatening shape. Before he could escape, Jason grabbed him and shot shaving cream up inside his costume. The white, lime-scented soap oozed down Ernest's neck.

"Hey, cut it out!" Ernest yelled.

His attacker fled, screaming delightedly, "Happy Halloween, Teeny-Weeny!" Then Jason, wearing authentic army combat fatigues and with nasty grease stripes painted beneath his eyes, bounded up the tallest slide to rejoin his laughing friends.

It took Ernest nearly fifteen minutes to clean himself up again. When he was certain no one else was nearby, he stuffed his costume inside the washroom garbage can. He couldn't wait for Halloween to be over. It was always one of the most dangerous holidays. This year, it seemed one of the loneliest as well.

He was greatly relieved when school ended. The

other children grabbed their Halloween costumes and masks and art projects and went happily leaping and yelling down the street. Wind blew the bare branches, and the air was soft and warm. It was perfect weather for trick-or-treating.

Ernest walked alone across the playground. He crumpled the silly construction paper pumpkin the art teacher forced them to make each year and the list of Police Department Halloween safety rules into his pocket. If only he were going trick-or-treating with a best friend, too!

Just as he reached the playground fence, he spotted Jomo, wearing a baseball jacket. This was Ernest's big chance. If he hurried, he could apologize about the Chococrunch bars and make Jomo realize he had not been tricked.

Jomo was whistling and bouncing a soccer ball into the air with his knee.

"Jomo!" Ernest called.

The ball flew up and careened into the street. Jomo dodged across just as the Number 201 bus rolled into view. By the time the bus passed, Jomo had sped halfway down the other side of the street, practicing pivot kicks.

"Maybe he didn't hear me," Ernest thought miserably as he continued walking home, "or maybe he really hates me."

When Ernest came home, he went straight to the basement. He felt comforted there, surrounded by his airplanes. He refused to go trick-or-treating.

"Oh, come and look, Ernie!" called his mother after dinner. She was wearing a purple bouffant Halloween wig that she thought made her resemble a famous Country and Western singer. She stood at the top of the basement stairs, holding a bowl of candy on one hip. "The little Sim twins are here. They're dressed like Tweedle Dee and Tweedle Dum, and they look so-o-o darling!"

Ernest groaned. He did not want to see the darling Sim twins. He did not want to see anyone.

"Aren't you going trick-or-treating tonight? You're missing all the fun. Why don't you come up here and put on your costume?"

"I'm busy, Mom!" he shouted. He thought to himself that life would be much better if he could just stay in the basement until he grew up.

CHAPTER

7

At recess after lunch the next day, Ernest watched a third-grade soccer game across the field. He was sitting on the ground several yards from Ben, who was carefully unwrapping caramel squares, flattening them into different shapes between his pudgy fingers, and then popping them into his mouth. Silently, Ernest poked a stick into the mud. He thought about how he had ruined everything with Jomo. Jomo would probably never speak to him again after the Chococrunch disaster.

A ball flew out of bounds and rolled nearby. Jomo ran swiftly after it. Ben, busy eating candy, did not even look up.

"You kick?" Jomo asked Ernest. "You want play?"

At first, Ernest was so startled that he hardly knew what to say. "You're not still mad at me about what happened yesterday with the chocolate bars? I didn't mean for you to get into trouble."

"Trouble? No trouble for me. Today I hide my candy good. See?" Jomo smiled proudly as he showed Ernest a handful of Halloween treats stuffed in his jacket pocket. "You want eat?"

"Thanks," Ernest replied, unwrapping a piece of bubble gum. He could hardly believe Jomo was actually standing right there, smiling, sharing candy, and inviting him to join his soccer team. It might be fun to play soccer with Jomo. Maybe everything wasn't ruined after all. Maybe people could have misunderstandings and still be good friends.

He could hear the other boys shouting and making loud, rude noises. "Let's go, Jomo!"

"Kick the ball over here!"

"Don't talk to that runt!"

Ernest hesitated. Finally, he shook his head. "No. Maybe another time."

Jomo shrugged. He expertly dribbled the ball back to the game.

Ernest stood up and brushed the seat of his pants. He broke a stick hard across his knee and wandered past the jungle gym to the drinking fountain. Dangling from the jungle gym bars were Sheila and her friends.

"Yooo-hoooo, Ernie!"

"Look, he's polluting the water!"

The bell rang, and everyone began running back to class. The soccer players pushed and shoved each other across the field. Jomo hurried to the drinking fountain. He was thirsty, too.

"Hey, don't drink that water!" Sheila shrieked.

"Ernie's been here!" Emily screamed. "You want Ernie germs?"

Jomo looked puzzled. He did not understand what all the trouble was about. He took a long drink and wiped his sweaty forehead with the back of his hand.

"Ernie germs! Ernie germs!" Jason chanted, dancing around Ernest.

His friends were holding their sides and laughing. "Jomo's contaminated!" Etherial yelled. "He's got Ernie germs now!"

Somebody grabbed Ernest's baseball cap and

threw it high in the air. Jomo scowled. He gave Sheila a fierce look.

"Don't anybody get near Jomo!" Sheila screeched. "He has Ernie germs!"

"Ernie germs! Ernie germs! Ernie germs!" the other girls sang.

Jason was pushing Ernest back toward the brick school wall. The black commando grease stripes left from the night before made Jason's face look more evil than ever. Ernest was so scared he accidentally swallowed his gum.

All at once, the pushing stopped. The girls' chanting stopped. Jason stood motionless.

There was Jomo, his face grim and threatening. He stood between Ernest and the wall, staring directly into Jason's eyes. "Cut it out!" he said in a low, menacing voice.

Jason's face didn't look quite so frightening anymore. The cruelness around his mouth was gone. Ernest thought he saw his lip quiver. "OK. OK. I'm not doing nothing!" Jason said, backing toward the school door and the safety of his friends. "See, look! I didn't even touch the little runt!" He motioned grandly to his friends and strutted back into school smiling, trying to appear unafraid. But everyone could tell he was only pretending. Jason was scared of Jomo.

"Come on. We're going to be late," Sheila whispered. She ran inside. The other boys and girls followed, gazing backward with curiosity, fear, and respect at the strange new boy and at Ernest, the third grader no one had ever thought worth befriending.

Jomo picked up Ernest's baseball cap, brushed it off, and handed it to him. "Come on. OK?"

"OK." Ernest smiled. The two boys walked back into the building together. They didn't say anything more to each other, but it didn't matter. Ernest felt amazed and grateful. Nobody had ever done what Jomo had just done for him. Nobody had ever taken his side in a fight.

At that very moment, Ernest decided he would do something very special for Jomo. Something better than inviting him over. Something better than just a Chococrunch bar. He'd give him a real present, the way friends did. He'd give him the model of the F-5F Tiger II.

CHAPTER

8

Ernest began final touches on his model as soon as he came home from school. Slowly and patiently, he positioned the decals "Lt. James Snake," "Lt. Quinn JJ," and "LCDR Conaster White Shoes." The names even sounded like friends, he decided. When the decals were dry the next day, he'd apply the last coat of paint to give the camouflage an authentic, dull finish.

This had to be the best model he had ever built in his life. He wanted it to be perfect for Jomo.

At first, Ernest did not even hear his mother come home from work. "Ernie darling," she called from the top of the stairs the way she always did, "what do you want for dinner?"

Ernest did not have a chance to answer. The phone rang.

"Ernie!" she called again. This time her voice was higher pitched. "The call's for you."

Ernest put down his paintbrush. It must be a wrong number, he thought, as he trudged up the stairs to the kitchen. Nobody ever telephoned except his father on Ernest's birthday. But today was not Ernest's birthday. Who could be calling?

"Please hurry! It's important!" his mother whispered, her hand over the receiver. Now that she was home from A-1 Plate Glass Company, she was wearing her comfortable fuzzy slippers that looked like dust mops. On the counter was a diet chocolate cream soda with plenty of ice.

The taut, worried expression on his mother's face frightened Ernest. He did not want to take the phone. "Have you been in trouble today at school?" she hissed, thrusting the receiver into his hands. "I think it's the principal."

Ernest's knees went rubbery. His mouth felt dry. Mr. Momaday must have found out about the pushing incident with Jason. Ernest panicked, wondering if Jomo was in trouble, too. "H-h-hello?" he said, his voice cracking. "Yes, this is Ernest speaking."

Mr. Momaday sounded different on the telephone than he did at school. He spoke very quickly, and his voice seemed friendlier than when he made announcements over the intercom or shouted into his bullhorn on the playground. "Ernest, sorry to be bothering you during the dinner hour, but I wanted to be the first to congratulate you."

"M-m-m-e-e?" Ernest stuttered in confusion.

Mr. Momaday chuckled. His laughter troubled Ernest. Maybe this was some kind of cruel joke. Maybe he wasn't really talking to the principal at all. Maybe this was really Jason or Etherial pretending to be Mr. Momaday.

Ernest's mother peered at her son with growing concern. She wanted to know why Ernest looked so scared.

"The wonderful news," Mr. Momaday continued, "is that you have officially won the All-School Balloon Send-off. And the remarkable thing is the way you won. I want to keep that part a surprise. I'll just say that I received a letter today from a boy who lives on a farm in Indiana. He recently found your balloon's card."

Ernest was so pleased that he was practically floating in the air.

"What is it? What is it?" his mother whispered. "It isn't bad news, is it?"

Ernest shook his head. He was smiling.

"In fact," Mr. Momaday continued, "it's such a remarkable story, the people at WBON-TV News are going to send a camera crew tomorrow morning to tape our school assembly in your honor. I just got off the phone making the arrangements. Think about it! After I finish reading this young man's letter, you'll be seen by millions of television viewers. WBON-TV is even broadcast by satellite to South America. Aren't you excited?"

Ernest collapsed into a kitchen chair. He felt as if he might throw up. An assembly in front of the whole school! He'd be standing there, all by himself on television, with Jason shouting some gross insult just as Mr. Momaday was about to announce Ernest's prize. Instead of being the laughingstock of Lincoln School, he'd now be the laughingstock of the whole world.

"Hello? Hello? Hello? Are you there? Hello?" Mr. Momaday's tiny voice kept repeating into the air. Ernest's mother grabbed the dangling receiver from Ernest's limp hand. "Mr. Momaday, this is Ernie's mother, Estelle Clark. Yes, I'm fine. Can you please tell me what's going on?" She nodded and listened. Her face glowed with pride.

Ernest couldn't believe it. Here was his mother, overjoyed that he was about to be publicly humiliated before millions of viewers. The class runt. The third-grade teeny-weeny. It was all too terrible to imagine. But of course, she wouldn't understand. She never did.

"Goodbye, Mr. Momaday. And thank you. Thank you very much," Mrs. Clark fluttered happily as she hung up the phone. "Can you believe it, Ernie? Why didn't you tell me about the balloon send-off? And of all those balloons, yours was the only winner. Aren't you excited? Just think, you'll be on television tomorrow."

"I don't want to be on television," Ernest mumbled. He wondered how anything that had started out so wonderfully could end up so badly.

"I'm so proud of you! I can hardly wait to tell everyone. All the neighbors, your Aunt Lor, your Aunt Marge, and all their children," his mother said, as if she had not heard him. She busily positioned a package of sugarless gum and her favorite nail file near the phone. Whenever she'd be talking for a long time, she always chewed and did her nails.

Ernest looked at his mother helplessly. How could he make her understand that winning the balloon send-off was his worst nightmare come true? He remembered the time he tried to get out of Little League. She had refused to listen then, too, somehow convinced that he was just as athletic as his father. Ernest had told his mother again and again that he was simply not interested in sports, that he could not survive daily after-school games with angry parents and teammates hooting in the bleachers every time he struck out. But she had not heard anything he said, and she had signed him up. Times like these had convinced Ernest that his mother must be nearly deaf.

"By the way, Ernie, who are you going to invite to go along with you for the pizza?" she asked. Her finger was poised to begin dialing every number she could think of.

"Mom, don't call me Ernie. Call me Ernest," he said slowly, turning the basement doorknob.

"All right, whatever. Who are you going to ask?"

"I have to think about it," he replied, shutting

the basement door behind himself. He walked slowly down the steps, contemplating yet one more dreadful thing he'd have to do tomorrow.

Who in the third grade would go with him to Pizza Roma? He could ask Jomo, but there was always the grim possibility that he'd refuse. Jomo had accepted the Chococrunch bars. He had shared his Halloween candy and had invited Ernest to play soccer. He had even protected him on the playground. But that didn't mean that Jomo wanted to be friends. After all, lots of people at school liked Jomo. He didn't need Ernest. And what if he turned down Ernest's offer in front of everyone at Lincoln School? In front of the television cameras! Then everyone everywhere—even Aunt Marge and Aunt Lor and his father in California—would know that he, Ernest Clark, had absolutely no friends.

CHAPTER

9

"Rise and shine!" Ernest's mother announced brightly the next morning as she flung open his bedroom curtains.

"Mom, I don't feel good," Ernest replied, coughing dramatically. He struggled up on one elbow and fell back onto his pillow. He hoped he looked green.

"Mr. Momaday just called to make sure you'll be in the auditorium on time. Wasn't that nice of him? You don't look sick to me. You look wonderful. Ernest, honey, this is your big day!"

Ernest stared at his mother in amazement. He could scarcely believe what he'd heard. She had just called him by his real name for the very first time. He rubbed his eyes and examined her carefully. Could this really be his mother?

"Now get out of bed and eat the nice, hot breakfast I made to surprise you. I've taken the day off from work just to see you win that prize at the school assembly."

Ernest groaned. There seemed no way out of his awful fate.

He arrived on the playground with a full, queasy stomach. He felt even worse when he noticed a panel truck in the parking lot. It had *WBON-TV* painted in big letters on the side and some kind of dish-shaped transmitter on the roof. The television camera crew had already arrived, and the transmitter looked powerful enough to reach at least halfway across the world. He was doomed.

Ernest walked slowly past the jungle gym claimed by Sheila and her friends. He was astonished when no one shouted anything at him. No one whispered. And he was even more surprised when out of the corner of his eye, he spotted Emily waving in a friendly way.

"That's him! He's the one!" a kindergarten boy in the hallway told his friend, pointing to Ernest. "I know him 'cause he lives on my street."

"Ernest!" Mr. Momaday exclaimed, hurrying to meet him. The principal shook Ernest's hand vigorously. "I'm glad you're right on time. Come into the auditorium so that we can make sure the lighting's right. You know, just a little rehearsal."

Ernest's palms were sweating. He tried not to look at any of the staring students as he hurried behind Mr. Momaday's squeaking shoes to the auditorium.

Bright camera lights had been set up near the stage. A short TV reporter in a tight suit with big shoulders was testing his microphone and giving directions to a cameraman wearing a baseball cap. The lights were so bright and so hot that Ernest could hardly breathe. He shielded his eyes from the glare.

For a moment, he was paralyzed. What if he had worn the wrong shirt this morning? He had once heard that TV performers never wore blue—or was it stripes? He tried smoothing his hair and hoped desperately that he had remembered to zip his pants all the way.

"Come right over here, young fella." The man with big shoulders motioned in a friendly way for Ernest to move to the center of the stage. "My name's Brett. Now, don't be scared. This isn't going to take long. Let's see a smile. Aren't you happy?"

Ernest tried to smile.

"That's better. How does that lighting look now, Irv?" he asked the cameraman. Ernest noticed that Brett's face was a strange, even color. He looked closely at Mr. Momaday and noticed his face looked the same. Ernest wondered if they were both wearing makeup. He hoped they wouldn't make him wear makeup, too. What if he couldn't get it off?

"When I'm finished, Irv will signal and the camera will shift to you, Mr. Momaday. I want you to stand over here when you read the letter and present the Pizza Roma certificate to Eddie."

"Ernest. My name's Ernest," Ernest said weakly.

"Ernest. Right. Ernest. Now, what else have we got?"

"The friend," Mr. Momaday spoke up. "Ernest is going to select a friend from Lincoln School to go with him to Pizza Roma. Isn't that right, Ernest?"

"Y-y-y-es, sir," Ernest mumbled.

"OK. We'll pan the audience. Maybe if we have time, Irv, we'll pick up a shot of the friend, too. We can try having the kids shake hands. Got it?"

Irv nodded and opened a new piece of chewing gum. He didn't look worried at all. And why should he? Ernest thought. Irv was on the other side of the camera. The safe side.

"All right," Brett said briskly, checking his watch, "I hope we're starting on time. We've got another tape to shoot across town after this."

"Of course we'll be on time," Mr. Momaday assured him. "The students are going to arrive any moment." The principal looked happy. He was finally going to be on TV.

As Ernest watched in sinking dread, the kindergartners and first and second graders began filing into the front rows of the auditorium. They were followed by the upper grades. Because of the TV lights and camera, there was an air of nervous anticipation in the room. Even the teachers looked excited.

Mrs. Delacorte smiled and waved to him, forming the "OK" sign with her fingers for good luck. He recognized his mother, wearing her good leopardskin coat, standing in the back of the auditorium with Aunt Marge. They waved, too. But he pretended not to see them.

Once everyone was seated, Mr. Momaday made a brief announcement. "Before we begin, I want you all to make me and Lincoln School proud this morning. You're going to be seen on WBON-TV Six O'Clock News tonight. I expect each and every one of you to be on your very best behavior."

Everyone cheered and clapped. Mr. Momaday raised his hand to quiet the happy chattering. Immediately, the room became silent.

"Follow Mr. Momaday's signal that very same way during the taping," Brett boomed into the microphone, looking pleased. "And when your principal goes like this with his hand in the air, I want to hear a big cheer. All right? Let's practice a few times."

Mr. Momaday raised his hand, and the students cheered. He lowered his hand, and the room became silent. Then he raised and lowered his hand again to let the children practice applauding and being quiet one last time.

The cameraman gave a cue to Brett, who glanced hurriedly at his notes on a pad of paper. Another bright light went on.

Brett grinned broadly and announced in a clear, resonant voice, "WBON is coming to you from Lincoln School in Buffalo Heights with the scoop on some airborne adventures. One month ago, every student at Lincoln attached a card with his or her name, school, and school address to a balloon released during a big send-off. Three hundred and four balloons suddenly filled the sky. Today marks the contest's last day. More than a dozen people have written to Lincoln to say they've found students' cards. But the balloon that went the farthest—255 miles—belongs to third grader Ernest Clark. He's being honored by his classmates in a special assembly.

"Here's Lincoln principal Leon Momaday to read a letter telling about Ernest's balloon's remarkable adventure."

This was Mr. Momaday's big moment, his wish come true. At last, he was appearing on television. He smiled nervously into the camera. Clearing his throat, he raised a piece of paper in one hand. His voice quavered as he began reading:

"Dear Ernest:

"I'm writing you because I found your letter. If it didn't drift the farthest with your balloon, then it had to have had the most exciting journey of any of the other balloon

71

letters. I found your letter when I was getting ready to feed our cows some more hay this morning.

"The thing about it was, a cow was eating your card. She bit off the corner. Your letter, Ernest, drifted into one of our fields of hay about seven miles away from our farm. It was mowed up, raked, packed into a hay bale, and brought to our house to be put into our hay barn.

"Today was your note's lucky day to be found. If it wasn't for my pet cow, Wilma, it could have been lost forever—"

"There you have it," Brett interrupted. "A cow named Wilma was about to eat the winning card when it was discovered by an eighteen-year-old farm boy in southern Indiana.

"Ernest, how do you feel about the fact that your balloon outdistanced every other one in the send-off?"

"I feel really wonderful. Very happy," Ernest said, tightly gripping both hands together so no one would notice how much they were shaking. "I never thought I'd win."

"Now tell us, who are you going to invite to share your prize, a free dinner offered by one of our sponsors, Pizza Roma?"

The camera began panning the audience. A few students waved. "I'd like to invite . . ." Ernest hesitated, "Jomo Mugwana."

Mr. Momaday signaled for everyone to cheer. Mrs. Delacorte crawled over the row of students to whisper quickly to Jomo. Ernest held his breath.

Jomo immediately jumped to his feet. He was grinning as he hurried to the stage. All around him third graders were cheering wildly. Ben was whistling with two fingers in his mouth. Even Jason, Etherial, Sheila, and Emily were applauding and waving at the camera. Ernest sighed with relief.

"Lucky! Lucky!" someone chanted, patting Jomo on the back as he made his way to the stage. The cameraman quickly shot Ernest and Jomo together and then the crowd in the auditorium.

Ernest hardly heard or felt anything that happened after that. It was like a dream. Now he was shaking hands with Brett, the TV reporter. Now he was shaking hands with Jomo. Now he was shaking hands with Mr. Momaday, who presented the

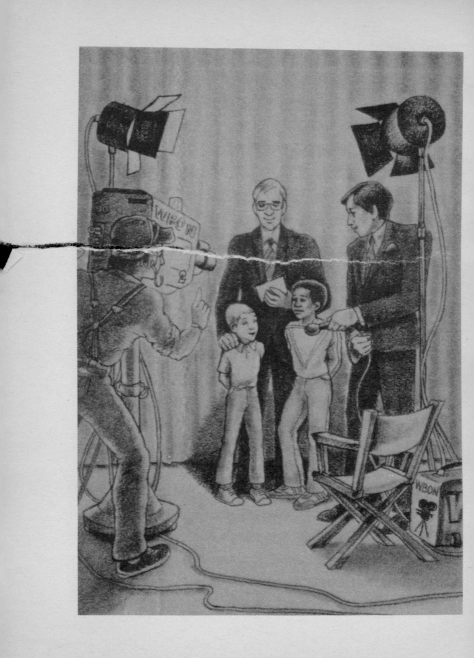

Pizza Roma certificate and the letter from Dana, Indiana. Everyone congratulated him.

It wasn't until the auditorium was empty and the camera crew had gone that Ernest had a chance to look more carefully at the letter. That's when he noticed Mr. Momaday had not read the ending.

"I am an eighteen-year-old graduate of Williams Junior-Senior High in Dana, Indiana. I don't know how you like school, but take it from me, they really are the best years of your life. Do the best that you can, and you will probably make out OK.

"I have really enjoyed writing to you. It's been a unique experiencc. Ernest, why don't you write to me and tell me something about yourself?

"Your Balloon-Letter Returner,
Eric Kent"

He straightencd his shoulders and glanced at the letter again. "Ernest, why don't you write to me and tell me something about yourself?" He smiled. He was not Ernie. He was not Runt. He was not Teeny-Weeny. He was Ernest Clark. Maybe he and Eric Kent could be pen-pals. Maybe he'd even send him one of his drawings. Eric Kent might like that.

It all seemed so amazing. What he had dreamed had finally come true. His balloon, soaring high above Lincoln School, had taken him someplace he had never been before. And best of all, he had found *two* friends.

Carefully, Ernest folded the letter and tucked it into his back pocket with his Pizza Roma gift certificate. "Thanks, Wilma the cow. Thanks, Eric from Indiana," Ernest announced in a confident television-reporter voice to the dark, empty auditorium. "Thanks a lot. This really is my lucky day."

CHAPTER

10

Jomo liked pizza. He had never eaten it before, but he liked it. "Want more?" he asked Ernest, pushing the second pan of cheese, mushrooms, green peppers, and anchovies across the checkered tablecloth at Pizza Roma.

Ernest wondered if he'd be able to fit in the car if he ate another slice. Sitting back, he thought about the trip to the restaurant. Not once did his mother call him Ernie or embarrass him in front of Jomo. His balloon-letter returner, Eric Kent, had promised things would be OK. Maybe everything was going to be better than OK from now on.

"I'm stuffed!" Ernest replied. He took the last bite of his sixth piece.

"Stuff. What's stuff?"

"It means full. I can't eat anymore." Ernest

puffed out his cheeks with air and patted his stomach.

"I'm stuff, too," Jomo said and made a face. They both laughed and laughed.

"You looked pretty good on TV tonight, Jomo," Ernest said, remembering that Jomo had smiled on the screen as if this were the best day of his life.

"I'm glad you pick me," Jomo replied. "I like TV. I like pizza. I like America. I like you, too."

Ernest felt completely happy. "There's one more surprise," he said. "I brought it in this bag."

"A surprise? I like surprise."

From beneath the table, Ernest pulled out the shopping bag he had carefully packed that afternoon. He removed the newspaper padding. There was the F-5F Tiger II model. "It's for you, Jomo. I hope you like it."

"You make this?" Jomo whistled, carefully examining the sleek jet fighter from all angles. "For me?"

Ernest nodded.

"It very good. Very good." Jomo held the model up to the light and made it climb in a slow, graceful arc.

"I have a whole collection at home that I've built myself. Prop planes, bombers, tactical fighters. All different kinds."

"Can I see?"

"Sure."

"Ernest, you teach me?"

"OK. I could show you how to make a model. That would be fun. Maybe after school tomorrow. You could come over to my house. We could walk home together. We could have a snack, too."

"OK. I come," Jomo replied. He poured Ernest another glass of root beer from the pitcher on the table. He picked up his glass, clinked the rim against Ernest's, and said, *"Harambee!"*

"Haram-bee!" Ernest repeated.

"You speak Swahili pretty good!" Jomo laughed and clinked glasses again. *"Heri na afya njema ndugu yangu."*

"What does that mean?"

"Good health, good fortune, and we friends for all times."

Ernest smiled. He felt as if he were floating above the clouds, beyond the moon, beyond the sun.

About the Author

LAURIE LAWLOR survived third grade and went on to major in journalism at Northwestern University. She has been a free-lance writer since 1977. Her Minstrel titles will include *Addie Across the Prairie* and *Addie's Dakota Winter,* both to be published in 1991. She is married and lives in Evanston, Illinois, with her two children.